Amanda Peace

Bob, the Tiny Dinosaur!

Bumblebee Books

A CIP catalogue record for this title is
available from the British Library.

ISBN: 978-1-83934-522-7

Bumblebee Books is an imprint of
Olympia Publishers.

First Published in 2023

Bumblebee Books
Tallis House
2 Tallis Street
London
EC4Y 0AB

Printed in Great Britain

Dedication

Dedicated to my husband Chris, my wonderful children Sophie and Alex and my mum who never gives up.

A long time ago, in a world far away,

there lived a dinosaur so tiny,

that he could be blown away by

a rustle of the wind or the sneeze of a boy.

Bob was his name and he looked just like a toy.

Bob was so little, he could fit into a shoe.

His tail was flame orange, his eyes twinkled bright blue.

Teased by the
others, scared to join
in with their fun.

He would
watch from the
side as they played
in the sun.

For he
lived in a
world where
size was the thing.
The biggest dinosaur
around was the one that
they called King.

All the herd were enormous, huge and giant beasts.

Spending their days
eating feast after feast.

But this is the story of Bob's **strong** belief,

that he could rescue his friend from a cave full of teeth.

Despite his small stature and his fear of the rain.

He knew he could help if he just used his brain.

Bob did have one friend,
named Betty May.
She was a large Stegosaurus
and they would spend every day,

playing hide and go seek
and singing their songs.

Until one day when it all ... just ... went wrong!!

Betty May got stuck
in a cave by the sea and
she soon discovered
it had plans for
its tea!

"Help, help, it's going to eat
meeeeeeeee!"

For the cave was a monster,
with teeth sharp and white
and those who went near it,
would soon feel it's bite.

Poor Betty May chose
this venue to hide
and now she was stuck
in the monster's inside.

The rest of the herd came
running to help

"Get me out, get me out!"
They could hear their friend yelp.

They pushed at the teeth, they pulled at the jaw,
but they all ended up in a heap on the floor.

Then Bob ran over,
a clever plan in his head.
"There's a gap in those teeth,
I could crawl through" he said.

The others just laughed,
"what a silly idea!"
But they did move aside and
they left the path clear.

Bob found a stick
which he tied to a vine.
Gave the end to the King
and said, "hold tight
to this line".

He squeezed and he squeezed
through the gap in the teeth,
til he emerged on the inside,
with a sigh of relief!

After hugging his friend,
he positioned the stick
along the back of the teeth.
"This would soon do the trick"

"Pull the line, pull the vine"
tiny Bob gave a shout.

The others pulled hard and the
friends both flew out.

Now Bob was a **hero**,
loved far and wide.
The herd now
looked at him
with awe and
with pride.

He was their good friend,
no matter how small!
But Betty May
loved him,
most of all!

And as for the monster
after that fateful game.
Well, you could say, his smile
was never the same!

Acknowledgements

Thanks to my husband for his continued support in everything that I do. Thanks also to my children for their insistence that I exercise my imagination by making up stories at bedtimes. Finally, thank you to my first primary school class who encouraged me to follow my dream of making Bob into a book.